THE STORY OF
MISS MOPPET

BY

BEATRIX POTTER

Author of
" The Tale of Peter Rabbit," etc.

LONDON
FREDERICK WARNE & CO., LTD.
AND NEW YORK

ORD EDN ISBN O 7232 0612 O

PRINTED IN GREAT BRITAIN FOR THE PUBLISHERS
BY HENRY STONE AND SON (PRINTERS) LTD., BANBURY
D·6338·980

THIS is a Pussy called
Miss Moppet, she thinks
she has heard a mouse !

THIS is the Mouse peeping
out behind the cup-
board, and making fun of
Miss Moppet. He is not
afraid of a kitten.

THIS is Miss Moppet
jumping just too late ;
she misses the Mouse and
hits her own head.

S HE thinks it is a very
hard cupboard !

THE Mouse watches Miss Moppet from the top of the cupboard.

MISS MOPPET ties up
her head in a duster,
and sits before the fire.

THE Mouse thinks she is looking very ill. He comes sliding down the bell-pull.

MISS MOPPET looks worse and worse. The Mouse comes a little nearer.

MISS MOPPET holds her poor head in her paws, and looks at him through a hole in the duster. The Mouse comes *very* close.

AND then all of a sudden
— Miss Moppet jumps
upon the Mouse !

AND because the Mouse has teased Miss Moppet — Miss Moppet thinks she will tease the Mouse; which is not at all nice of Miss Moppet.

S HE ties him up in the duster, and tosses it about like a ball.

BUT she forgot about that hole in the duster ; and when she untied it — there was no Mouse !

HE has wriggled out and run away; and he is dancing a jig on the top of the cupboard!

The "PETER RABBIT" BOOKS
by BEATRIX POTTER

PETER RABBIT · SQUIRREL NUTKIN
TAILOR OF GLOUCESTER · BENJAMIN BUNNY
TWO BAD MICE · MRS. TIGGY – WINKLE
MR. JEREMY FISHER · TOM KITTEN
JEMIMA PUDDLE-DUCK · THE FLOPSY BUNNIES
MRS. TITTLEMOUSE · TIMMY TIPTOES
JOHNNY TOWN-MOUSE · MR. TOD
PIGLING BLAND · SAMUEL WHISKERS
THE PIE & THE PATTY-PAN · GINGER & PICKLES
LITTLE PIG ROBINSON

A FIERCE BAD RABBIT   MISS MOPPET
APPLEY DAPPLY'S   CECILY PARSLEY'S
  NURSERY RHYMES   NURSERY RHYMES
      *
  PETER RABBIT'S   TOM KITTEN'S
  PAINTING BOOK   PAINTING BOOK